KT-419-885

WITHDRAWN

C334318166

For Fuffy

SIMON & SCHUSTER
First published in Great Britain in 2017
by Simon and Schuster UK Ltd
1st Floor, 222 Gray's Inn Road, London, WC1X 8HB
A CBS Company

Text and illustrations copyright © 2017 Sue Hendra and Paul Linnet

The right of Sue Hendra and Paul Linnet to be identified
as the authors and illustrators of this work
has been asserted by them in accordance with
the Copyright, Designs and Patents Act, 1988

All rights reserved, including the right of reproduction
in whole or in part in any form

A CIP catalogue record for this book is available
from the British Library upon request

978-1-4711-2103-6 (PB)
978-1-4711-2105-0 (eBook)

Printed in China

5 7 9 10 8 6

SUPERTATO

RUN, VEGGIES, RUN!

by Sue Hendra and Paul Linnet

SIMON & SCHUSTER

London New York Sydney Toronto New Delhi

It was night-time in the supermarket but Supertato and the veggies were going for the burn.

"Come on, veggies, you can do it!"

"To keep fit of course! Whoever heard of an unhealthy vegetable?" Supertato grinned.

"Just look at yourselves!
It's time we got you fruit and veggies into shape."

Supertato thought for a minute. "I know - let's have a sports day!" he said.

Everyone groaned.

"There'll be prizes . . ."

Everyone cheered!

"ATTENTION!" shouted Supertato as they all limbered up. "It's time for the first events. Running and jumping and spinning.

Asparagus, you can be the starter."

GO PEPPER!

Then suddenly the ground shook.

"Oh no," said Cucumber. "It's **The Evil Pea!**"

Everyone gasped. The Evil Pea was grinning.
"Gloria here wishes to enter your competition," he said.

"A pleasure to meet you, Gloria," said Supertato.

CRUSH OPPONENTS
WIN PRIZES WIN PRIZES
PRIZES PRIZES

"Hmmm,"
thought Supertato.

"Ok, let's start the race.

Carrot, you're in lane one,
Broccoli lane two,
Cucumber lane three,
Gloria . . . you can take four, five and six.

Over to you, Asparagus."

"They will never defeat my robot," sniggered The Evil Pea. "Those prizes are as good as mine!

Mwah ha ha ha ha!"

BROCCOLI RULES!

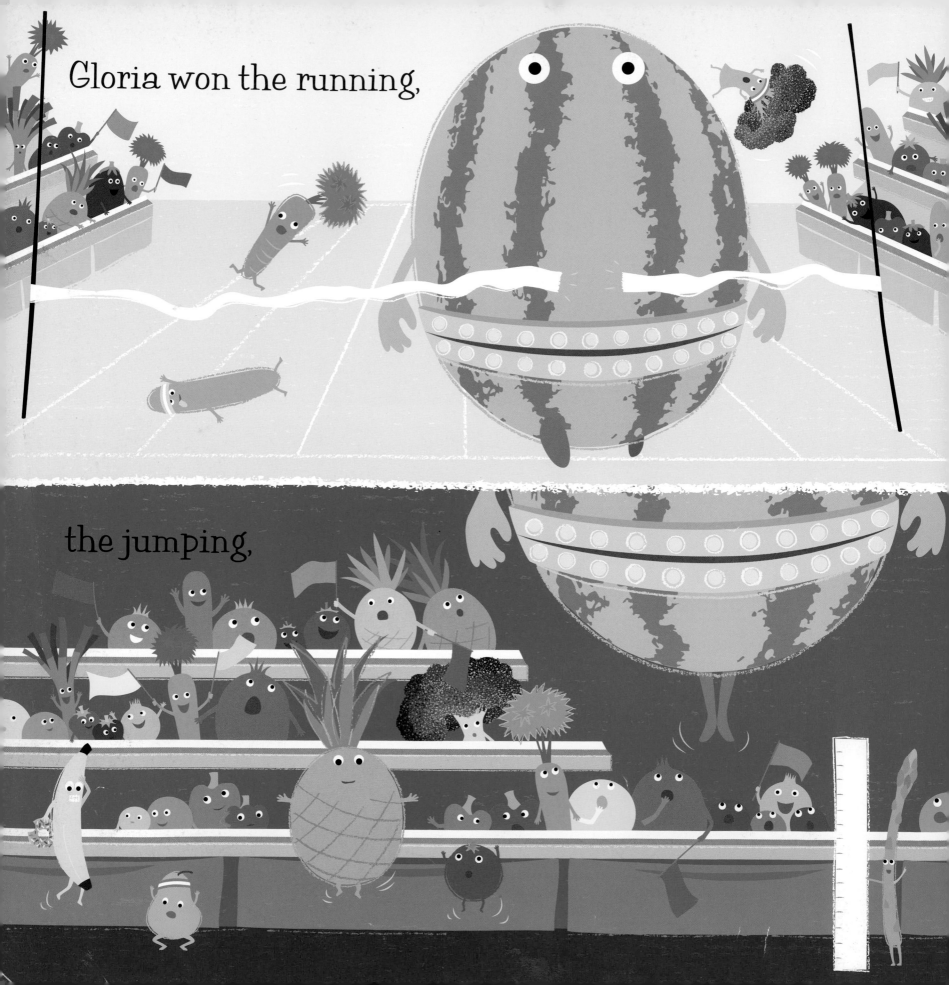

Gloria won the running,

the jumping,

the spinning,

and the lifting of heavy things.

In fact, she won
everything!

"Time to be off, Gloria,"
said The Evil Pea.
"We have all the prizes,
our work here is done!"

"Well, actually," said Supertato,
"there's one more event to go . . .

... SWIMMING!"

MUST WIN PRIZES
CRUSH WIN

"STOP!" shrieked The Evil Pea. "I don't think you should be doing any swimming, Gloria.

You're not really a **water** melon!"

But it was too late. "And they're off!" shouted Asparagus.

Gloria was well in the lead . . .

...but then she started crackling and sparking...

... and juggling!

He scooped up the swimmers and took them to safety.

"Hurray for Supertato!"

But just as Supertato flew back in to deal with the melonbot . . .

... IT EXPLODED!

"Is this the end for Supertato?"
panicked the pineapples.

NOT THIS TIME!

"It's a good thing we've seen the last of that naughty melonbot . . ." said one fish finger to another.

WIN PRIZES

ZZZZZ I'LL BE BACK . . .

"Oooh," said The Evil Pea, "time for a 100 metre dash."

"Not so fast, Pea. There are no prizes for cheating.

It's back to the freezer for you!"